USBORNE SCIENCE & NATURE
ANIMAL BEHAVIOUR

Felicity Brooks

Edited by Corinne Stockley

Designed by Stephen Wright

Illustrated by Chris Shields and Ian Jackson

Additional illustrations by Joseph McEwan

Scientific advisors: Dr. Margaret Rostron and Dr. John Rostron

●Contents

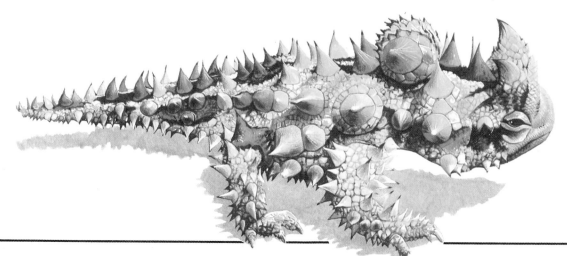

First published in 1992 by Usborne
Publishing Ltd, 83-85 Saffron Hill,
London, EC1N 8RT, England.

Copyright © 1991 Usborne Publishing Ltd.

The name Usborne and
the device 🎈 are the
Trade Marks of Usborne
Publishing Ltd.

Printed in Spain

About this book

The scientific study of the behaviour of animals is called ethology. This book explains some of its basic ideas and principles. Understanding animal behaviour takes a great deal of of time, patience and careful observation and the knowledge we have today is the result of detailed studies done by researchers over long periods of time. Some of the experiments that they have designed to investigate behaviour are described in the book, along with accounts and explanations of the behaviour of individual species.

The development of ethology

People have always observed the way in which animals behave. Early man depended on wild animals for food and needed a knowledge of their movements and behaviour in order to hunt them successfully. Observation of wild animals also helped people tame species such as cattle and sheep that were useful for food, and to train others such as dogs and horses to perform tasks.

Ethology as a science, however, is quite a recent development. Konrad Lorenz and Niko Tinbergen (see page 46) are generally considered to be its founders. They placed great emphasis on the observation of animals in the wild. Other scientists have worked more with animals in laboratories to find out how they learn and what motivates and affects their behaviour.

Now ethologists are investigating many different fields. For instance, they are using knowledge gained from the study of animals to try to shed light on human evolution and behaviour, and also to help in the conservation of animals. We need a detailed knowledge of the behaviour and ecology of endangered species if we are to protect them successfully.

Important people

Some important people in the world of animal behaviour are mentioned in this book. You can find out more about them on page 46.

Using the glossary

The glossary on page 47 is a useful reference point. It brings together and explains many of the terms used in the book.

These greater birds of paradise are performing a courtship display. You can find out more about these displays on pages 34-35.

3

Instinct and learning

All animal behaviour contains elements of instinct and learning. Instinct can be thought of as internal "programming", which all animals have because of the type of animal they are. Baby lambs, for example, do not gape and chirp like baby birds, and baby birds do not search for a teat to suck in the way that lambs do (see right). Each young animal is "programmed" for its own particular type of behaviour.

Learning begins as soon as an animal is exposed to the outside world. Its senses are bombarded with stimuli and it must learn to respond to these in the right way. As it grows, it is exposed to more and more stimuli and gains more experience. It constantly adapts and adjusts its behaviour to respond to these new experiences. This is the process of learning. These are some examples of behaviour which show both instinct and learning.

Baby birds gaping to be fed

Lamb drinking milk

A young squirrel with its first nut seems to know instinctively that the nut should be cracked open. However, its first attempts at cracking it open are clumsy and aimed at the wrong part of the nut. The exact skill is only gradually learned with practice, after which the nuts are cracked open in a matter of seconds.

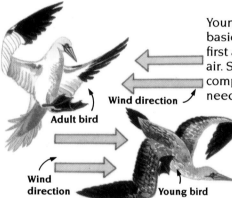

Young birds can carry out the basic flying movements at the first attempt, and stay in the air. Some of the more complicated manoeuvres need to be learned and practised though. For example, at first they are often not very good at landing.

Wind direction

Adult bird

Wind direction

Young bird

Young birds must learn to land into the wind.

First nut opened by young squirrel in a test

Several nuts later

Instinctive learning?

Imprinting is a special process which takes place in the first, crucial days of the lives of many newborn animals, such as some birds and mammals. It has sometimes been thought of as instinctive learning, that is, a mixture of the two elements discussed on these pages. The new-born animals "fix upon" the first large moving object they see (a parent) as the one which they will recognize and follow around from that moment on. This is an inborn device to help them gain protection from their parents. It can be said that the new-born animal is internally "programmed" to learn to recognize its parent.

In his famous work with greylag geese, Lorenz* showed that if a man was the first large, moving object seen by newborn goslings, they would imprint on him and follow him around.

Experiments have shown that even things such as balloons can be made the object of imprinting.

*See page 46

Wasp test

After a female digger wasp has emerged from a pupa and mated, she immediately performs a complicated series of acts which seem to be internally "programmed". She digs a burrow, carefully seals the entrance and flies off to catch a caterpillar.

On her return, she re-opens the burrow, puts the caterpillar inside and lays an egg on it. She carries out this series of actions a number of times. (The caterpillars are food for when the eggs hatch.)

Wasp returning with caterpillar and re-opening burrow.

Digger wasp

Closing the burrow for the last time. She has stocked it with caterpillars, and laid her eggs on them.

The learning aspect of this behaviour comes in each time the wasp returns to her burrow. Experiments by Tinbergen* showed that a wasp learns the position of her burrow by memorizing local features, such as stones and twigs. This is vital, as there are often many burrows close together.

While a wasp was away hunting, Tinbergen moved several landmarks. The wasp was very confused when she came back, taking 20 minutes to find her burrow.

He then placed a ring of pine-cones around the burrow and waited a few days for her to fly around and memorize these new landmarks. Then, while she was away, he moved the ring a little to one side.

When the wasp returned, she flew straight into the middle of the ring, missing the burrow completely.

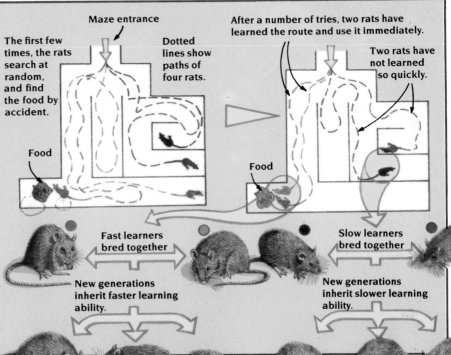

There is another fascinating aspect to the ideas of instinct and learning. Experiments have shown that an animal's genes influence its ability to learn. That is, some animals are internally "programmed" to be better learners than others.

Experiments with rats in a maze showed that some were quicker at learning the route to hidden food than others. When the fast learners were mated with each other, their babies proved to be fast learners too. When the slow learners were mated, their babies proved to be slow learners. Breeding animals in this way for a specific genetic reason is called selective breeding.

Maze entrance

The first few times, the rats search at random, and find the food by accident.

Dotted lines show paths of four rats.

Food

After a number of tries, two rats have learned the route and use it immediately.

Two rats have not learned so quickly.

Food

Fast learners bred together

Slow learners bred together

New generations inherit faster learning ability.

New generations inherit slower learning ability.

*See page 46

Different types of learning

A growing animal is constantly coming across new situations in the outside world. It has to adapt to all of these situations in order to survive. As it keeps on developing and changing its behaviour to react to the new situations, it is learning all the time. You can find out more about the various different ways in which animals learn on the following six pages.

Fallow deer

Habituation

Habituation is a simple, common type of learning. It is shown when an animal becomes less sensitive to a stimulus. It gradually reacts less and less to it, and eventually does not react at all. This is because it has "got used to" the stimulus. It has found that there are no benefits to be gained from reacting to it, or dangers from not reacting to it. Habituation occurs in many situations in the wild, such as with deer.

Deer grazing on verges close to roads have got used to, or become habituated to, cars speeding past and not stopping. They have learned that the cars do not present a threat to them. If a car did stop, the deer would run away. They are habituated to one situation, but this does not stop them reacting differently if the situation changes.

Habituation can also be seen in the behaviour of birds when faced by a scarecrow, or other bird scarer. Farmers and gardeners know only too well that unless the appearance, or sound, of a bird scarer is changed regularly, birds will soon learn to ignore it.

Scarecrows are often unsuccessful.

Habituation is very important to all animals, including humans. It enables us to filter out stimuli that need a response from all the other stimuli that bombard our senses. We would be in a constant state of tension if we reacted to every sight, sound or other stimulus we received.

Spatial learning

It is important that animals learn the layout of their home territory. This is called spatial learning.

Almost every animal explores its home area as a baby, or, if it comes into a new area, as an adult. It finds out about food and water sources, and the best routes from one place to another. If an animal did not do this, it would have to search at random for food and water every time it came away from the nest or den, and find its way back by searching at random as well.

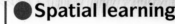

If a rabbit is frightened, it runs straight to its burrow – it does not have to retrace its steps or search at random.

Path of rabbit

By exploring a home area at first, but also then by being active in the area and "taking in" information subconsciously, an animal builds up a fund of knowledge about the area. This is an example of latent knowledge – knowledge which an animal has, but which it may not necessarily use immediately.

Latent learning

We all have latent knowledge about the area we live in. At first, we have explored, and found the best routes to the various places. But we have also "taken in" information without actively learning it. This is called latent learning.

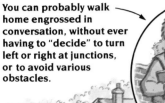

You can probably walk home engrossed in conversation, without ever having to "decide" to turn left or right at junctions, or to avoid various obstacles.

You can probably walk around a room at home with your eyes shut or in the dark, avoiding all the furniture. But did you ever sit down and learn where the furniture was?

Route home

Wide arc to avoid bush

You may have learned the actual route while exploring, but you have also "taken in" a lot more information. For instance, you may make a wide arc around a bend to avoid a bush which sticks out just around the corner.

Try moving a kitchen object, such as a toaster, to a different work surface. How many times do people in your family go to the wrong place?

They have taken in the position of objects in their surroundings so well that they are ignoring messages from their senses about the new position of the object.

Ignoring messages

Many pieces of behaviour are not just the result of one type of learning – they are influenced by many types. The toaster example above, for instance, shows aspects of habituation as well as spatial learning. Although a stimulus is received from the eyes, it is ignored, because the person has got used to not having to look for the object every time.

An experiment carried out by the American scientist Donald Griffin showed that animals can also get so used to messages from their own senses that they ignore them.

Original layout of barriers

Flight path of bat

A bat was allowed to get used to flying a particular route through a dark room. It avoided the barriers by listening to the echoes of its own high-frequency squeaks coming back off them. When the layout was changed, the bat took its usual route and flew straight into a barrier. Although still sending out squeaks, it had got so used to the same echoes coming back, it had stopped listening to them and so did not notice the changed echoes of the new layout.

New layout of barriers

It took a number of tries, and crashes, before the bat found a new route.

7

Different types of learning (continued)

●Learning by association

The term learning by association, or associative learning, covers a wide range of learning. Generally, it is shown when an animal learns to associate (link together) two or more sets of circumstances or stimuli. This leads it to change its behaviour, often to bring about a specific result, or to avoid this result. In most cases what happens at first is a series of events known as "trial and error" after which the association becomes fixed in an animal's brain. Some examples of associative behaviour in the wild are described below.

Birds of prey often return to places where they have hunted successfully. (The places become associated with food.)

Golden eagle

Site of successful hunt

A bird may try to eat cinnabar moth caterpillars. It soon learns to avoid them, however, as they taste nasty. It has learned by trial and error. The caterpillar's colours become associated with the taste, so the bird then avoids eating anything of the same colour.

Cinnabar moth caterpillar

Many animals associate noises or smells with particular things, such as the imminent arrival of an enemy. They will react by preparing to fight or flee.

This gazelle has just caught the scent of a lion.

● Experiments to show associations

The idea of associative learning was first shown by a number of laboratory experiments with animals. The animals were "taught", or at least induced, to form associations in their brains. The term "conditioning" has often been used since then for this way of producing associations.

Earlier in this century, Pavlov* conditioned a dog to salivate whenever it heard a bell ring. Of course, the dog did not do this to start with, but Pavlov always rang a bell just before feeding the dog.

At first, the dog only salivated when it saw or smelled food. Eventually, though, just the sound of the bell was enough to start it salivating. It had learned to make an association in its mind between the sound of a bell and the arrival of food. You may see examples of associative learning in household pets.

Many cats react to certain noises, like a fridge door opening or a knife chopping food. They associate these sounds with being fed.

A dog may get excited if you put on your coat, or rattle any chain that sounds like its leash. It associates these sights and sounds with a trip outside the house.

*See page 46

●Searching images

An animal is said to have acquired a searching image if it actively looks for one particular item, such as a type of food, and ignores other items. Having found that this type of food tastes good, it forms a mental picture of it from visual aspects. It associates this image with the taste. It ignores similar things that may be as good, because it has not encountered them yet, and has not made an association in its mind.

If a bee in search of nectar first finds it in a pink flower, it will often acquire a searching image and associate pink flowers with nectar.

Bee

This bee is flying only to pink flowers although there are flowers of different colours close by. It will only try other colours after trying all the pink ones.

You can see if any birds acquire searching images by using food colouring to dye pieces of bread different colours. Scatter the bread outside and see if any species of bird make colour associations.

Coloured bread

Bread

Food colouring

What colour do the birds first eat? Do they then look for this colour and ignore others?

Searching images are especially interesting with relation to camouflage (see page 24). If an animal, such as a bird, comes across camouflaged prey, such as a caterpillar, its ability to "pick out" other camouflaged creatures of the same type increases. This is because it has acquired a searching image.

Grasshopper

You may acquire a searching image if you are looking for particular animals, such as grasshoppers in a field. Once you have seen one, you suddenly see others much more easily.

If you stare at a cluttered drawer of cutlery, you can normally pick out the item you want, even though it may be "camouflaged", i.e half-hidden, and the same colour as other items. This is because you have a searching image of the item in your head.

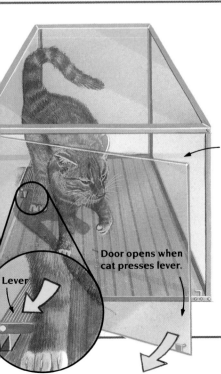

Door opens when cat presses lever.

Lever

In another experiment, Thorndike* used a box with a lever in it, and showed how a cat can learn to press the lever, in order to open a hatch and escape from the box.

The first few times, the lever was pressed by accident (as the cat frantically tried to escape).

However, the cat soon associated pressing the lever with escaping, and began to press it on purpose.

Skinner** later did similar experiments with a variety of animals, using boxes with levers inside (such boxes are now known as Skinner boxes). He did several with rats and a lever that opened a door to reveal a morsel of food.

*E.L Thorndike – American scientist   **See page 46

Different types of learning (continued)

● Imitation

Imitation is a form of behaviour whereby animals learn to do things by copying other animals in their group. It happens a lot as baby animals grow up and learn from their parents, or through play, about coping with the world around them. It can also happen with adult animals.

Imitation is linked to learning by association (see pages 8-9). Animals, especially when young, try to imitate the actions of others, but do not necessarily get the right result. For example, though young birds appear to have an internally "programmed" model of the song of their species in their heads, it is only a very basic one. It has to be perfected by imitation.

Studies of chaffinches have shown that, at first, they sing a crude version of the adult song, with notes of roughly the right length and pitch, but no more refined than that. Only after listening to the adult song for a period of time can they produce it accurately themselves. They have learned by imitation.

Sonograms are charts on which sounds are represented visually. They are used in the study of bird song and other sounds made by animals.

Chaffinch singing

Sonogram of song of young chaffinch

Sonogram of song of mature chaffinch

● Imitating Imo

A famous example of imitation involved a troop of Japanese macaques (a type of monkey) studied in the 1950s by scientists. The scientists scattered sweet potatoes on a beach to entice the macaques out of the forest to feed. After a period of time, they noticed that the troop had developed a new habit – they were taking the potatoes to the sea and washing the sand off before they ate them.

Macaques washing sweet potatoes

Macaques "sieving" grains

Later, the scientists began to leave wheat grains on the beach, which the macaques had to pick delicately out of the sand one by one. Soon the macaques were picking up handfuls of sand and grains, and throwing them on to the surface of the sea. The sand sank and the wheat floated, so they could easily scoop up the clean grains.

Over a number of years, these techniques became commonplace in most of the troop and were seen to spread by imitation. In both cases, members of the troop were imitating one young female macaque (the scientists called her Imo) who had "invented" both techniques. She probably hit on them by chance (by dropping a potato or grains in water by accident), although it may have been insight (see box opposite).

● Blue tits

Another example of imitation involved blue tits. In the 1920s, 30s and 40s, a habit spread through the blue tit population of Great Britain. A few birds had found that piercing the foil top of a milk bottle left on a doorstep, revealed a meal underneath. Many other birds imitated this technique, and soon it spread around the country.

The first "inventor" blue tits probably found half-open bottles, or broke the tops by accident. They learned by chance, but soon began to break the tops on purpose. Other birds then imitated the actions.

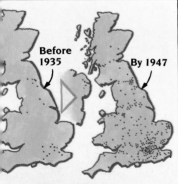

Before 1935   By 1947

Blue tits were first seen opening milk bottles in southern England in 1921. The maps show reported sightings before 1935 and by 1947.

● Insight

Insight is regarded as the highest form of learning and many people believe that only humans are capable of it. Experiments have been done with "higher" animals, such as apes and monkeys, but it is difficult to prove that they also possess this ability.

Insight occurs when a solution to a problem appears to be found by a process of reasoning without obvious "trial and error" learning. Mental associations and knowledge acquired in other situations are used in this process.

If you wanted to climb up to a window, you would fetch a ladder. You reason out the solution using knowledge you possess (you associate ladders with getting higher up).

An experiment was carried out with chimpanzees to try to prove that they were capable of insight. It involved presenting them with a bunch of bananas too high to reach, a pile of boxes and some sticks which fitted together to make longer sticks. The chimps contemplated the boxes and sticks and then seemed to arrive at the correct solutions.

Some chimps piled up the boxes, so they could climb up to reach the bananas.

Some chimps fitted the sticks together so they could reach up to knock the bananas down.

It was easy to conclude that the chimps had reasoned out their solutions, using their previous knowledge of boxes and sticks (through play, they had learned how boxes could be piled up or sticks fitted together).

However, other people pointed out that they could just as easily have been playing, and have accidentally solved the problem of reaching the bananas.

Chimpanzees in the wild have also been said to show insight. Goodall* has described how they make simple tools, such as carefully prepared twigs, to help them obtain food.

Most of the chimps seen to use tools are probably imitating others, but even with the original "inventors" of techniques, it is difficult to prove insight, as it is with Imo the macaque or the "inventor" blue tits. The solutions to the problems may have been "reasoned out", using knowledge acquired in other situations, but it is also possible that the techniques were hit upon by accident.

Chimp using a prepared twig for probing a termite nest and extracting termites to eat.

*See page 46

11

Aggression

Aggression, or aggressive behaviour, in an animal is the act of attacking or threatening to attack another animal. It is used to try to gain control of resources, such as a place to live, a mate, or food. Most aggression is shown by males, but females do show it sometimes, for instance when defending young.

Animals rarely fight. Instead, most disputes are settled by threatening displays. Both animals in a dispute try to frighten the other off, using noises and signals designed to show how strong they are. This is a safe trial of strength – the animals can "size each other up" without risking injury. The disputes usually end with one animal fleeing or signalling submission. At the beginning of a dispute gaping, roaring or bellowing is very common. Many animals also take up threatening postures.

Male red deer roaring

Hippo gaping →

← A black-headed gull strikes a threat posture by standing very upright with its beak pointing downwards and its wings held slightly out.

If not settled by the first threats, the dispute continues in stages, with different signals. Each new stage means a greater level of aggression (see right).

Territories

Many animals compete aggressively to gain "ownership" of an area of land, or territory, and then to defend it from challengers. The territory normally contains certain vital resources such as good breeding sites.

The males of many bird species compete in the spring for territories with good access to food and nest sites. They then try to attract a mate.

After roaring, red deer pace up and down next to each other. This is called parallel walking. →

Rattlesnakes wrestle, trying to push each other to the ground, instead of using their fangs.

Fighting

If all else fails and neither animal backs down, fighting may occur. Generally, the more important the object of the aggression is to both animals, the more likely it is that they will fight. For instance, if a resource is scarce, there will be more animals competing for it, and so greater levels of aggression. Even when animals do fight, many stick to specific, almost ritual, forms of fighting, which are less likely to cause injury.

Many animals have body protection against serious injury, and blows are always aimed at these areas on their opponents' bodies.

Male elephant seals slash with their teeth at their opponent's neck and shoulders. They are well protected here by extra-thick layers of fat.

Deer lock antlers and push against each other in a contest of strength, instead of trying to spear each other's sides.

Most territorial disputes only happen at certain times of year, usually during the breeding season. Nearly all take place at the edges of territories where challengers first approach.

Territory holders often signal their ownership in some way.

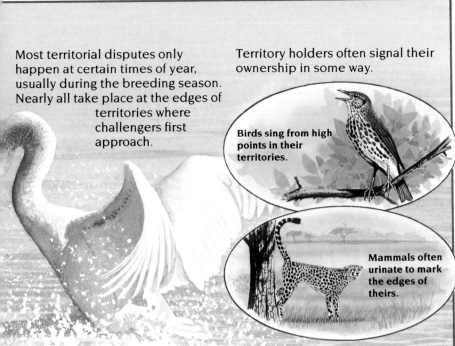

Birds sing from high points in their territories.

Mammals often urinate to mark the edges of theirs.

Anti-predatory aggression

This type of aggression is shown in the face of a real or imagined threat from a predator. When protecting young, for example, individual mothers or a group of animals will threaten to attack, or actually attack, another animal which comes too close, even if it intends no harm.

Birds often collectively attack a predator, such as a hawk, which flies into their area. This is called mobbing.

Group aggression

Animals that live in a group may defend a collective territory against intruders. This depends on the size of the group – for large, mobile groups, such as herds of deer, territories would be impossible to create or defend. Such animals may not compete for territories, but still use aggression in other cases, such as for the right to mate with females.

A group territory, such as that held by a pride of lions, is often more permanent than an individual one.

In smaller, more closely-knit groups (social groups), such as those of many apes, a "pecking order" of importance can be seen, where a dominant animal has priority over all resources, from mates to "first bite" at food. Other animals are ranked below this top level. An animal constantly uses varying levels of aggression to assert and maintain its rank.

The term "pecking order" was first used of hens.

Dominant hens assert superiority by pecking subordinate (weaker) ones.

In social groups, it is important that the winner and loser of a dispute stay "on speaking terms". The group would soon split up, and the benefits of group living (such as collective defence) would be lost if every loser ran away. Instead, group members display "I am running away", or submission, signals which show they are beaten, but let them stay in the group.

Wolves and dogs roll on to their backs with their tails between their legs, in a posture of total submission.

Conflict behaviour

Many types of behaviour are the result of a conflict inside an animal – it is "torn" between two sets of internal stimuli. For instance, aggressive signals show that an animal is caught in a state of tension between an urge to attack and an urge to flee. "Frozen" postures and parallel walks are examples of conflict behaviour.

Some animals break the tension with irrelevant acts, such as birds suddenly preening feathers. This is called displacement activity.

Some animals redirect their hostility. For instance, deer may thrash at vegetation with their antlers. This is called redirected response.

Conflict behaviour can be seen in humans, for example, taking up threatening postures or hitting tables instead of other people.

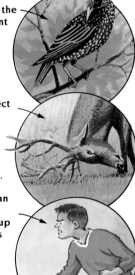

Migration

Many animals migrate, or travel between one habitat and another, to make use of different or superior resources, such as better food supplies or warmer and safer places to breed. Most migrations happen once a year during particular seasons, but others occur more, or less, frequently. Although necessary, these long journeys use up a lot of an animal's energy and time and expose it to many dangers such as exhaustion and lack of food.

All sorts of species migrate, from whales to tiny insects. Migrant species tend to use the same routes every year. The routes vary from species to species. Swimming and flying animals travel furthest.

The longest migrations of all are made by Arctic terns. They fly from their breeding grounds in the Arctic to the Antarctic and back each year – a round trip of about 36,000km (22,000 miles).

Migration allows Arctic terns to enjoy 2 summers a year and a plentiful food supply.

Bird migrations

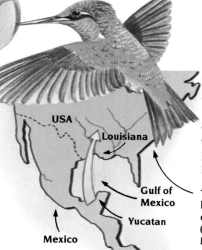

Many birds make regular seasonal migrations. In the spring, they fly from areas with a warm winter and a good food supply to cooler regions where they breed and rear their young. These cooler regions have a plentiful food supply only in spring and summer.

Twice a year, tiny ruby-throated hummingbirds fly across the Gulf of Mexico, a distance of 800km (500 miles) between Yucatan in Mexico and Louisiana, USA.

Some species, however, migrate to a place with little food, but which offers protection for breeding and rearing young. Animals return to these breeding grounds year after year.

Adélie penguins travel over 300km (186 miles) of rough sea ice to reach their breeding grounds on the Antarctic mainland. The same pair of penguins will return to the same nest site every year.

Herd migrations

In regions such as the African plains and the Arctic tundra, food and water are scarce for much of the year. Herds of animals move with the seasons to make best use of available resources.

As the dry season approaches in one area, enormous herds of wildebeest travel long distances across the Serengeti plains in Tanzania, Africa in search of food and water.

Movement of gazelle, wildebeest and zebra

Serengeti National Park

In Canada, caribou spend the winter in conifer forests. In April, they migrate north to the tundra (the treeless Arctic region) to breed and feed on lichens and grasses. They return to the forests as the Arctic winter begins and the ground becomes covered in a hard layer of ice.

Migrating caribou are followed by grey wolves. The wolves hunt down young and sick animals which cannot keep up with the group.

Caribou

Grey wolf

14

More seasonal migrations

Whales move from feeding grounds to breeding sites and back again each year. From November to April, Southern Humpback and Blue whales feed on tiny animals, called krill, in polar regions. As winter approaches, they swim into the Atlantic, Pacific and Indian oceans to breed in the warm tropical water.

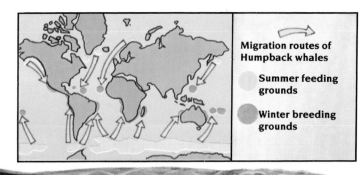

Migration routes of Humpback whales

Summer feeding grounds

Winter breeding grounds

Young whales do not have to use up as much energy keeping warm in tropical water as they would in polar water.

Frogs, toads, newts and salamanders all breed in fresh water, but spend most of the year on land away from these sites. Each year they return to the streams and ponds where they were born in order to breed.

Green tree frogs in eastern USA migrate from the trees to their breeding ponds and back.

● Monarch migrations

In autumn, millions of monarch butterflies migrate from northern USA and southern Canada to spend winter in the milder climate of California or Mexico. They may travel up to 4,000km (2,480 miles).

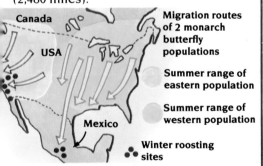

Canada

USA

Mexico

Migration routes of 2 monarch butterfly populations

Summer range of eastern population

Summer range of western population

Winter roosting sites

Those that survive the winter start to move back north to breed. During the summer months as they move north, as many as five generations may live and die. Each generation moves further north. Those born in late summer begin to move south again as days grow shorter.

New generations of monarchs, in search of food and warmth, fly back to the same roosting sites every autumn.

● Monitoring migration

Scientists use a variety of methods to track the movements of migrant species, including radar and satellite monitoring.

Scientists can recognize individual birds by ringing their legs. This helps them to work out species' migration patterns.

Large animals such as polar bears can be fitted with radio transmitter collars whilst under sedation.

Radar screens can show the movements of large flocks of birds.

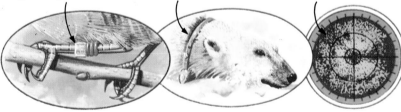

●Irruptive migrations

These migrations only occur irregularly. They happen when conditions have been especially good for breeding (such as mild winters with plenty of food). This brings about a population explosion and great competition for resources. This may, in turn, trigger a one-way migration of some animals, in search of better conditions, to areas in which the species is not usually found.

A well known example of irruptive migration is seen in lemmings, small rodents usually found on mountain tops and in the Arctic tundra. When the migrations occur, hordes of lemmings move across the country and may even reach the sea.

Norwegian lemmings

Navigation and orientation

Navigation is the process of finding the way from one place to another. Orientation is knowing one's position in relation to other animals and objects in the environment. Animals need these skills to be able to steer a course during migration, to find food, to follow trails or just to get home. They rely on a wide variety of senses to navigate and orientate, including sight, smell, hearing and sensitivity to heat and light. Some of their methods are still not fully understood.

Navigation by smell

A tracker dog's nose is so sensitive it can follow a trail by sensing substances called fatty acids present in human sweat. We deposit tiny amounts of sweat on the ground, even when we are wearing shoes.

The olfactory membrane (the part concerned with smell) in a tracker dog's nose has 220 million sensory cells.

Salmon also use smell for navigation and orientation. After spending a few years in the ocean, they find their way back to the stream where they were hatched, to lay eggs. When they approach the estuary leading to their "home" stream, the salmon recognize and swim towards the stream's unique smell – a mixture of dissolved minerals, decaying plants and animal life.

If an enemy, such as a bear, enters the water further upstream, the salmon can smell it and stop their migration.

Salmon have to swim against the current and struggle up waterfalls to arrive back at their birthplace.

Arthur Hasler, an American scientist, did an experiment to show how salmon navigate. He collected and tagged 300 salmon which had arrived back at their birthplace and blocked the nostrils of half of them.

He released all 300 back into the main river, downstream from their birthplace. Those with unblocked nostrils headed back to their home stream. Those with blocked nostrils had lost their sense of direction.

Nostrils

Home stream

Main river

Hasler's experiment

300 salmon released he[re]

Using electricity

Some fish send rapid pulses of electricity into the water, creating an electrical field around their bodies. Anything coming into the range of this field causes distortions in its lines of force and can be detected by the fish. In this way the fish can find prey and avoid obstacles.

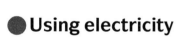

Lines of force in electrical field surrounding knife fish.

Object distorting lines of force

Fish that use this system must avoid distorting their own lines of force. They have to keep their bodies very straight. They swim using one long, undulating fin.

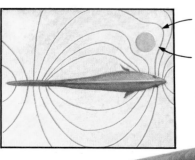

Knife fish

Using heat

Rattlesnakes use the two small pits in their heads to detect the body heat of prey. At the bottom of each pit is a skin with 15,000 heat-receptive cells. These can sense any object whose temperature is only slightly above that of the surroundings.

Side to side movements of the head help a snake find out how big the prey is.

Pit organ

The heat which an animal gives off can be detected by a rattlesnake even in total darkness.

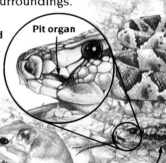

Rattlesnake

Sound systems

Insect-eating bats orientate themselves and navigate in the dark using a method called echo-location. They emit rapid squeaks (too high for the human ear to hear) as they fly. These reflect back from objects. By listening to the echoes, bats can detect prey and avoid obstacles.

Most echo-locating bats fly with their mouths open.

Bats usually send out only 4 or 5 exploratory squeaks a second. As soon as an echo comes back, the rate may increase to up to 200 a second.

Dolphins also use sound, emitting up to 700 clicks a second by forcing air through special passages in their heads. The returning echoes are also detected by a system of air spaces in their heads. Using this method, they can navigate and orientate to catch fast-moving fish in dark or muddy water.

Using the sun

Some birds can steer a course using the position of the sun. It seems that their brains can carry out complex calculations taking into account the sun's position at different times of day and of the year.

Kramer* did an experiment to show this, using starlings which were ready to migrate. The birds were put in a cage with six windows which let the sun in. Each window had a shutter with a mirror fixed to its inside surface. These could be moved to reflect the light and alter the apparent direction of the sun's rays.

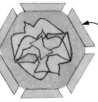

When the birds could see the sun, they faced north-west as if to start their migration.

Direction of sun's rays

When the sky was overcast and the sun was not visible, the birds showed no preference for any one direction.

When the direction of the rays was altered, the birds adjusted position to face what they now thought was north-west.

Mirrors altering direction of rays

Direction of sun's rays

*Gustav Kramer – German Zoologist

Using the stars

Many birds are able to migrate at night. An experiment done in Bremen, Germany, proved that they use the stars to navigate. It was performed inside a planetarium (a dome with an artificial night sky), using some blackcaps which were ready to migrate.

First the planetarium was lit to show the star pattern as it was at that time above Bremen. The birds took up a position facing south-east, as if to start their migration.

The whole pattern was then rotated 90° anti-clockwise. The birds adjusted their position with respect to the new pattern.

Using the Earth's magnetic field

Some birds can find their way on cloudy nights with no stars to guide them. It is believed that they can somehow sense the lines of force of the Earth's magnetic field and use them to orientate themselves. Recently, tiny pieces of magnetic material have been found in pigeons' skulls and necks. These may help them to sense the magnetic field.

Experiments with European robins in cages (from which the sky was not visible) showed this ability. When the direction of the magnetic field was changed artificially, the birds adjusted their position.

Pigeons can find their way home, even when released in unknown territory, far from their roosts.

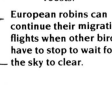

European robins can continue their migration flights when other birds have to stop to wait for the sky to clear.

17

● Communication

Communication is the act of sending out messages or signals to make known a fact, express a feeling and so on. Animals communicate for many reasons such as to attract mates, deter predators, show fear or to keep in contact with others. Some examples of different methods of communication are described on the following four pages.

● Body talk

Visual signals travel faster than sound, but most can only be seen over short distances. Many animals change the posture, colour or apparent size of their bodies to communicate messages visually.

● Facial expression

Some animals have a range of facial expressions. In wolves, six have been recognized: friendly, submissive, playful, very offensive, very defensive and aggressively offensive.

Wolf with friendly facial expression ←

An Australian frilled lizard will suddenly produce a collar to make its body look huge. This surprises predators and sends out the message "I am too big to eat".

As in humans, an animal's body posture can signal different moods. A greylag goose, for example, though it does call to show anger, depends mostly on body posture to express itself.

Attitude of alarm ↗
Inferiority ↙
Approach to prospective mate

Ring-tailed lemurs on the move keep their tails up.

Tails are very useful for communication. A pet dog wags its tail to show happiness or excitement, but a tail held between the legs may show dejection. Tail swishing in a cat, however, often occurs before an attack. In a group, tails may be held up as flags to keep group members together.

● Colour

Colour is an effective means of communication over short distances. It is used extensively, especially when trying to attract a mate or deter predators.

A male chameleon can change colour rapidly according to its mood. It displays bright colours and assumes a threat posture when faced by a rival.

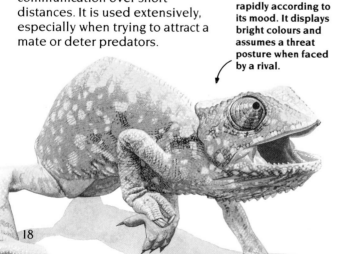

Squid and octopuses have a remarkable colour "language". It has been known for some time that they change colour according to mood – an octopus turns white when afraid, for example. Recent studies have shown that these changes are part of a complex language.

Changing patterns of colour sweep across a squid's body. More than 35 patterns have been recognized, combined in a great number of ways as part of the squid's language. →

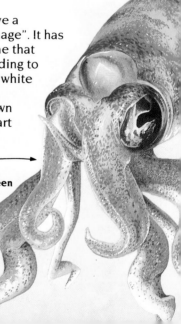

Chimpanzees often combine their facial expressions with gestures and sounds. Their expressions can easily be misinterpreted since they do not always correspond to our own.

We may wrongly interpret a chimp's expression of anger as "laughter".

●The dance language of bees

Group-living insects such as wasps, bees, termites and ants have highly-developed systems of communication involving touch, sound and smell as well as visual signals. Some species of honeybee, for example, communicate certain facts by "dancing".

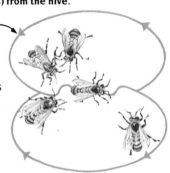

When a bee flies back to the hive having found a good source of food, she performs a dance. In 1944 von Frisch* discovered that parts of this dance tell the other bees the distance and direction of the food from the hive.

A round dance is used to show that the food is less than 80m (87 yds) from the hive.

●Light language

Light communication is useful at night and in the darkness of the deep ocean and of caves. Some animals make great use of it.

Fireflies are really night-flying tropical beetles. There are about 130 species. They signal by means of flashes of light. Each species has its own code, so members of the same species can recognize each other.

Some species of fireflies operate in groups. Thousands of males light up one tree, flashing with a synchronized rhythm to attract females.

A figure-of-eight 'waggle' dance is used when the food is more than 80m (87 yards) away.

During the middle part of this dance, the bee waggles its abdomen. The greater the number of waggles, the further away the food is. Each waggle corresponds to roughly 75m (82 yards) from the hive.

The direction of the food is shown by the angle of this dance in relation to the sun.

A female glow-worm cannot fly, but her light is brighter than a male's. She emits a steady greenish glow from the ground. Males can pick her out from a distance and fly towards her light.

Female glow-worm

Photoblepharon

Photophore

Photoblepharons are small fish. They have light organs called photophores below each eye. These lights can be turned on and off and are used to confuse enemies, attract prey and possibly to communicate with other fish.

If the food is exactly in the direction of the sun, the bee keeps the middle part of the dance vertical.

If the food is at an angle of 45° left of the sun, for example, the middle part of the dance will be at an angle of 45° left of the vertical.

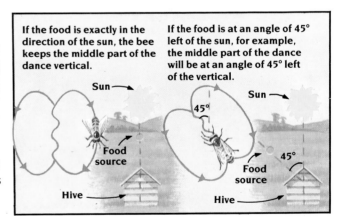

Sun →

45°

Sun →

Food source

45°

Food source

Hive →

Hive →

After the dance is over, the other bees fly off in the direction shown. A single bee can recruit many helpers in a short time. Sharing information increases the colony's food-gathering efficiency.

*See page 46

Communication (continued)

Sound and smell play an essential part in communication between animals. Sound can be used over long and short distances to communicate a variety of messages. It is often used alongside other methods of communication, such as body posture.

● Bird song

All birds produce calls which can register aggression, alarm, fear and so on, but only song birds (a group that makes up over half of all bird species) are able to "sing". Each species has its own song. The songs are used to deter rivals from entering territory and to attract a mate.

Scientists have noted that the greatest amount of singing is done in the breeding season and males sing more than females. In many cases individuals have their own variations of their species' song. The individuals which sing most variations attract mates first.

A male sedge warbler returns to Europe in April, establishes a territory and then sings almost non-stop until he attracts a mate.

Nightingales may be able to sing hundreds of different variations of their species' song.

● Keeping in contact

Sound is often used when animals cannot see each other but need to keep in contact, such as at night or in thick vegetation. In rain forests, howler monkeys call at dawn and dusk. Many species call in the day as well.

Howler monkey calling

Frogs croak mainly at night to defend territory and attract mates. Some species have large vocal sacs. These can be filled with air to act as resonators, increasing the volume of their calls.

A frog's vocal sac enables it to be heard up to ten times further away than a frog without such a sac.

● Whale song

Many whale species communicate by "singing" underwater. The songs that have been studied most are those of humpback whales, made up of sighs, squawks, roars, groans and chirps. Each song lasts up to half an hour and may be repeated for hours on end. It is estimated that the songs can be heard 1,200km (750 miles) away. The songs are only sung by unmated males and their exact function is still unclear. They may serve as locating signals or as claims to feeding grounds. Recent studies have suggested that they may be part of a sort of breath-holding competition. The length of the song may demonstrate a whale's status and fitness, helping females to select a mate by his singing ability.

Blue whales make the loudest noise of any animal. They sing underwater with moans of up to 188 decibels which may be heard 1,600km (1,000 miles) away.

Alarm calls

Animals living in groups have many quiet calls which pass between them as they move about. In addition, if a group is in danger, an alarm call is given by one or more members to warn the others. Alarm calls are usually short and loud.

Zebras utter a barking call.

Elephant talk

Elephants use smell and sound to communicate over long and short distances. Their calls include barks, roars, snorts and rumbles. Many rumbles are below the human range of hearing and are in what is known as infrasound. Males and females live apart for most of the year, but females need to inform males that they are ready to mate.

Several elephants freeze at the same moment with raised, spread ears to catch faint calls from up to 8km (5 miles) away.

This chart shows the pitch of calls emitted by elephants and various other species. Some animals' calls are in ultrasound which is above the human range of hearing.

Ultrasound

Human range of hearing

Shrews

Bats

Porpoises

Dogs

Birds

Insects

Frogs and toads

Blue whales

Crocodiles

Each line represents 1 octave

Elephants

Infrasound

Smell

Smell is a very important method of communication in the animal world. It can be effective over distances and over a period of time, as well as in the dark.

Most moths use smell to advertise for mates. When a female is ready to mate, she produces a perfume, called a pheromone. This is so strong that only a few molecules need reach a male moth for him to be able to locate her position.

An atlas moth's antennae can detect tiny quantities of a pheromone released by a female 2km (1.2 miles) away.

Mammals use smell to mark territory, attract mates, lay trails, and to drive away predators and rivals. Some species have special scent glands which they rub against objects to produce scent; others use urine or faeces. Other animals can "read" these chemical messages.

Male ring-tailed lemurs rub an unpleasant smell from a gland in their arms on to their tails so they can waft it towards a rival in a "stink" fight.

Deer and antelope mark territory by leaving scent marks from glands near their eyes.

Rhinos mark their territories, especially at the boundaries, with piles of faeces.

Foxes, like dogs, use urine to mark their territories. The scent probably indicates individual identity as well as how long ago the mark was made.

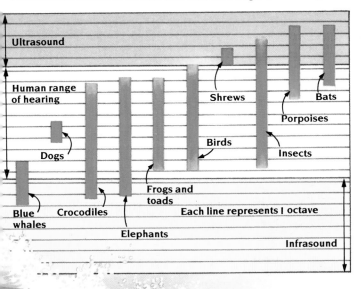

● Finding food

All animals must find an adequate supply of food to survive. They obtain their food in a variety of ways, from hunting other animals to growing fungus to eat.

Most methods involve the use of senses such as sight, smell and hearing, or special techniques, such as stealth or disguise.

● Hunting

Animals which depend mostly on hunting other animals for food are called predators. Hunting methods vary from species to species, but many rely on speed, strength or surprise to catch their prey.

Big cats, such as cheetahs, use stealth and speed when hunting. Cheetahs are the fastest land animals, reaching a top speed of 115km (70 miles) per hour.

A cheetah watches a herd of gazelles for a weak or small animal to pick off. Having selected its prey, it creeps up quietly in the long grass.

The cheetah accelerates to chase the prey. The chase is exhausting and usually lasts less than a minute.

If it catches up, the cheetah brings down the gazelle with its paws.

Gazelle

Less than half of these chases are successful. Young cheetahs may chase for too long, or are unable to bring the prey down. Even adults may time the

moment of acceleration badly. After such an attempt, a cheetah has to wait at least half an hour before it has recovered enough to try again.

A domestic cat also uses stealth to catch prey. It detects prey by sight and smell and then listens carefully to get a good idea of where it is. It creeps up, unnoticed, to make a rapid pounce.

When a cat detects a mouse, it freezes in a crouched position. The tip of its tail twitches in excitement and it keeps its eyes fixed on the area where the mouse is.

Excellent eyesight helps owls hunt at night.

Owls hunt at night and depend mainly on hearing to locate prey. They can pinpoint very accurately the sound of a mouse rustling leaves. When a victim has been detected, the owl swoops down silently to grab the prey in its claws.

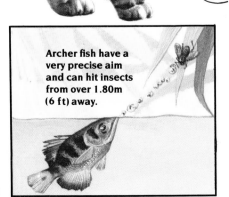

Archer fish have a very precise aim and can hit insects from over 1.80m (6 ft) away.

Archer fish live in the shallow waters of mangrove swamps and rivers. They shoot down insects from overhanging vegetation by spitting powerful jets of water at them. The fish practise this skill from an early age, becoming more expert as they get older.

Hunting in groups

Some animals, such as African wild dogs, hyenas and lions hunt in pairs or groups. Their prey is larger and/or faster than themselves, so a co-operative effort is needed to bring it down. All individuals in the group share the meal.

A pack of African wild dogs chases a zebra until it shows signs of tiring.

The dogs overtake and surround the zebra, attack it from all sides and tear it to pieces.

Storing and farming food

Many animals store food when there is a good supply and later use these stores, or caches, when food is scarce. This is known as cacheing behaviour. It can be seen in many insects, mammals and birds.

Squirrels store nuts by burying them. They are known to bury many more than they can remember, so some nuts end up as trees.

Honeypot ants have an unusual storage system. Some members of a colony, known as repletes, are used as living storage jars. Other worker ants feed honeydew and nectar to the repletes. This is stored in their abdomens which slowly swell until they are the size of peas.

Replete honeypot ants can do nothing except hang from the roof of an underground gallery inside their nest.

When the dry season comes and food is scarce, the active workers visit the repletes and caress them with their antennae until they regurgitate droplets of the liquid food for them.

Some insects such as termites, beetles and ants grow fungus gardens on plant material inside their nests. The fungus is used as food for adults and grubs.

These leaf-cutter ants are taking pieces of leaves to their nest. The pieces are chewed to encourage fungus to grow and then taken to a fungus garden.

Using tricks to catch food

Some animals have ingenious ways of catching food, involving lures, traps or mimicry.

Deep-sea angler fish have a luminous lure on the front of their heads. The waving of the lure tempts prey to come within reach of the fish's large jaws.

Lure

A trap-door spider makes a burrow with a lid of silk and soil. It waits inside with the lid half open. When an insect comes near, the spider springs out and grabs it.

This female firefly mimics the flashes that females of another species of firefly use to attract mates. When a male arrives, she eats him.

Food from plants

A large number of animals rely on plants for food, eating leaves, shoots, fruit or seeds. Some plants have ways of deterring animals: leaves may be surrounded by thorns or filled with poisons; seeds may also be poisonous or protected by hard cases. Nevertheless, animals have ways of overcoming such problems.

Gerenuks are long-necked antelopes which feed mainly on leaves. They stand upright and use their mobile lips to pluck out shoots from between sharp thorns.

Macaws sometimes gather in groups to gnaw soil. The minerals in the soil neutralize poisons which the birds absorb from the seeds they eat at certain times of year.

Avoiding being eaten

Many animals are in danger of being eaten by other animals at some point in their lives. They have all developed ways of lessening this risk. These range from avoiding being seen to escaping quickly. Some animals use a variety of tactics.

Escaping

Antelopes use agility and speed to escape from hunters. As they run they perform high leaps with all four feet leaving the ground at the same time. This is called stotting. It confuses enemies and may also tell them to look for less fit and active animals.

The antelopes that perform the most feeble leaps are more likely to be caught.

Camouflage and disguise

Many hunters rely on eyesight when hunting, so some prey try to avoid being seen by making their bodies blend into the background. This is called camouflage. It often takes the form of simple colour matching (a green insect in grass), or patterning which breaks up the outline of the body and matches the background.

Other animals disguise themselves as a particular object in their environment. Like all camouflaged creatures, they have to choose a suitable background and keep very still to avoid detection.

A crab spider can adjust its colour to suit its background and so can move between flowers of different colours. This camouflage serves mainly as protection from birds.

Horned frogs in the Malaysian rainforests have pointed hoods of skin over their eyes and a colour which allows them to merge with the dead leaves on the forest floor.

During the day, this praying mantis rests near leaves which it matches almost exactly.

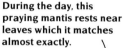

Adult thorn tree-hoppers in the jungles of Central America disguise themselves as green thorns. The young (called nymphs) look like rough, brown bark.

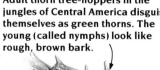

Flatfishes such as plaice can change colour to match their background. They also flick sand over their bodies to hide their outline on the sea-bed.

Body protection

Some animals have developed body protection in the form of hard shells, spines, and so on, to deter predators from attacking and eating them.

A tortoise could never rely on speed to escape, but is well protected by its hard shell. It tucks its legs and head inside when in danger.

An Australian thorny devil cannot outrun enemies, but its spikes provide good protection. It tucks its head between its legs and arches its back when attacked.

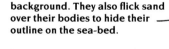

● Warning colours

Some animals use the opposite tactic to camouflage. They have brightly-coloured bodies, often patterned with orange, yellow or red markings and black or white stripes. They make little attempt to hide and are conspicuous and active all day. Their colours warn predators that this prey can sting, irritate, inflict a poisonous or painful bite, produce a bad smell, taste foul if eaten or is poisonous.

Predators quickly learn to avoid eating animals which display these colours (see page 8). If a bird gets stung by a wasp, it will then avoid not only wasps, but also any yellow and black animals, even ones which look nothing like wasps.

This Arizona coral snake is one of about 50 species of brightly-coloured coral snakes. Its markings warn that it is very poisonous.

Arrow-poison frogs can secrete poison from their skin. Their bright colours warn predators to keep away.

● Mimicry

Some animals which are harmless mimic (copy) the warning colours of dangerous species and so avoid being eaten themselves. This is called mimicry.

This sawfly is harmless, but gains protection by mimicking a wasp.

King snakes are not poisonous but their resemblance to coral snakes (see left) protects them from birds.

● Confusing the enemy

Many animals have ways of surprising or confusing their enemies. Their tactics may distract an attacker, divert its attention to a non-vital part of the body or surprise it so that it goes away. False "eyes", for example, are used by many species. Some butterflies and moths have them on their wings. A wing may be torn in an attack on the "eye", but the moth or butterfly still survives.

Some animals avoid being eaten by inhaling air or water to send out an "I am too big to eat" message.

An io moth spreads its top wings to reveal its false eyespots.

This hawkmoth caterpillar can change its body shape and use its eyespots to mimic a snake's head and scare predators.

This South American frog puffs itself up and pulls its legs in close to its body to make the best use of the false eyespots on its bottom.

When a puffer fish is in danger, it inflates itself to resemble a prickly ball.

Some animals pretend to be dead when in danger. This form of defence may deter predators such as lizards and cats which never strike to kill inactive prey, but not all hunters are put off by it.

Opposums feign death when attacked. This behaviour may result in a would-be attacker trying elsewhere.

A variety of animals can break off a non-vital part of their bodies when attacked. This surprises the attacker and gives the victim time to escape.

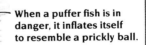

A young five-lined skink can break off its blue tail. The tail keeps twitching to confuse the predator.

The tail grows back in a few weeks.

● Aggressive defence

Some animals fight back when threatened. They may be armed with spines, teeth, claws, or smelly chemicals.

Many warn that they can retaliate before they do: porcupines rattle their quills; cats hiss and raise their fur. These displays may be enough to deter a predator without an attack being necessary.

Before squirting its smelly fluid, a spotted skunk warns a predator by performing handstands.

Co-operation

Co-operation, or co-operative behaviour, is behaviour in which members of a species join together in groups for activities such as hunting, defence or care of the young. There are many names for these groups, such as herds, colonies and troops. Some are temporary, only forming for a specific purpose. Others are permanent and closely-knit, with a clear structure.

Safety in numbers

Group living offers animals many advantages – it gives greater protection from predators and helps each member get food and mates, so increasing its chances of survival.

Brent geese form large flocks in the winter to feed on mudflats with a plentiful supply of eel-grass. This has the advantage that some can feed whilst others watch out for predators, and means that each bird can spend more time feeding than if it were on its own.

Brent geese in a feeding group are not related. The flock splits up at the beginning of the breeding season.

Other birds, such as gannets, form groups, called colonies, only for the breeding season. This increases each bird's chances of finding a mate. The birds nest in protected areas to lessen the risk of danger from predators. An alarm call from one bird can alert the whole group.

Gannets form huge cliff-top nesting colonies of up to 20,000 birds.

Shoal of snappers

Thousands of fish in a school swim side by side in the same direction. They speed up, slow down and turn together. Living in a huge shoal reduces an individual's chances of being eaten.

Many grazing animals, such as zebras and antelopes, live in large herds for safety. Predators do not usually attack the whole group but wait to pick off a solitary animal which is too old, young, or sick to keep up.

Within a herd, zebras stay in small family groups, usually led by one large male. He gives an alarm call if the group is in danger. The animals in the group always stay close to one another.

Zebras groom each other in pairs. In this way, both can keep a look-out.

Co-operative hunting

Some species, such as lions and chimpanzees, co-operate to obtain food, hunting in groups and sharing prey.

Lions are the only big cats which live in groups. Their groups, called prides, are made up of two or three lions and several lionesses and their young. The lionesses do most of the hunting, working in teams to outwit the herds of antelope and zebra which are their main prey.

Having chosen a victim, the team spreads out to approach it from different directions, trying to separate it from the herd. They then make a combined rush, or ambush it from a hiding place. If the hunt is successful, the kill is shared by the pride, the males having "first bite".

A wildebeest will provide a pride of lions with enough food for a couple of days.

● Sharing the care

Some species share responsibility for care of the young animals in their group. Flamingoes, for example, living in flocks of up to one million members, operate a baby-sitting system. While some are feeding with their heads in the mud, others watch the young.

Young flamingoes are kept among the long legs of a group of adults.

Ostriches also share the job of rearing young. A number of females lay their eggs in one nest. One pair of adults looks after the nest which may contain as many as 50 eggs. Not all hatch, but the one pair raises all the young that do.

A male ostrich looks after the nest at night. The female, who is camouflaged, takes over during the day when the male would be too conspicuous.

Within a herd of elephants there are a number of distinct family groups, each consisting of a female, her daughters and her grandchildren. Females born into a family group stay in it their whole lives. Males live apart from the herd, in their own groups, or by themselves.

When a baby elephant is born, females in the family group may assist at the birth, helping to clean the baby and lift it on to its feet for the first time. These young female helpers, called "allomothers", play an important part in the rearing of the babies.

Baby elephants receive a lot of attention. Their allomothers fondle them with their trunks, make sure they do not wander too far, play with them, wash them and protect them.

● Sociable meerkats

Meerkats are small mongooses which live in the desert in southern Africa. They live in tightly-knit groups in which all animals are related and of equal status. They share many tasks such as defence, care of the young and burrow digging.

Whilst the rest of the group feeds, one or two meerkats are always watching out for predators such as jackals, snakes and eagles.

A meerkat may be on sentry duty for an hour or more. A single alarm call can send the whole group underground.

Meerkats appoint baby-sitters to look after the young while the group is feeding. Baby-sitters also feed the young and teach them to forage. Each young animal attaches itself to an adult for instruction.

A baby-sitting meerkat guarding infants.

When on the move, group members stay close together. If a predator approaches when they are out of reach of their burrows, they stick together, raising their fur and hissing in unison. This can deter an enemy as large as a jackal.

Meerkats on the move keep their tails up and stay close together.

27

Co-operation (continued)

Some animals live in very tightly-knit groups, or societies, with complicated structures and clear hierarchies and rules, which each member knows and usually obeys. The most complex societies of all are those of certain insects, such as termites. Primates, such as baboons and gorillas, also live in highly-organized social groups and display a wide range of co-operative behaviour.

● Baboon troops

Savannah baboons live in troops of between about 20 and 100 animals. Each troop has a fixed territory. A troop's rigid social structure can most easily be seen when it moves out of the trees into the open country, as shown below.

At the top of the hierarchy are the large dominant males who are the leaders. They lay claim to the best "beds" in the trees, the most attractive females and the best food.

The strongest young males rank below the leaders. They enjoy some rights, but must recognize the superiority of the leaders.

The dominant males stay close to the mothers and babies in the middle of the troop, in order to protect them.

The strongest young males act as scouts, going out in front. They give the alarm call and threaten to attack if an enemy approaches.

Newborn babies cling to their mothers' chests.

Younger males guard the sides and back of the troop.

Females with young and those on heat (ready to mate) gather in the middle of the group.

Older babies ride on their mothers' backs.

Juveniles stay near the middle.

Other females travel nearer the edges.

Males leave the group at adolescence and then come and go between groups. This means that inbreeding (breeding with close relations) seldom occurs.

A female's status depends on her breeding pattern. Mothers and females who are on heat or pregnant are protected by the dominant males.

Babies receive a lot of attention from males as well as females. Grooming groups (see below) gather around mothers with young babies.

Juveniles (the more independent young animals) spend a lot of time playing in small groups, learning skills they will need later in life from games such as chases and fights.

Females who are not expecting nor rearing young stay on the outskirts of society. Most females spend all their lives with one troop.

● Grooming

When resting or feeding, baboons gather in small groups to groom each other. This helps strengthen friendships, partnerships and family ties as well as keeping fur clean. It is important for the health and security of the troop.

● Threat and submission

A dominant male will snarl at a rival of a lower rank who challenges his position. The rival will then usually take up a submission posture, presenting his backside. Only if he refuses to do this will he receive a bite on the neck.

● Baby baboons

Baboons normally give birth to one baby at a time. For the first few weeks, a baby clings to its mother all the time. At about four months it starts to become more independent and by ten months starts playing with baboons of its own age.

●Gorilla societies

Gorillas are shy and gentle animals. They live in family groups of about 12 animals. Each group is led by a large, silver-backed male. Gorillas spend most of their time on the forest floor, quietly feeding on vegetation.

The silverback is an old male who guards against intruders and sees off any rivals to his group.

Gorillas spend a lot of time grooming each other. This plays an important part in social life and helps hold a group together.

Communication is by gestures and facial expressions – a stare is rude and invites attack. Keeping the head low and the eyes down shows submission and friendliness.

A baby maintains continuous contact with its mother until it is about 4 months old. Mothers are very protective of their young.

The mothers with young spend a lot of time near the leader. He is tolerant of the young gorillas and will baby-sit infants for short periods.

Most animals stay with their home group for at least eight years. Males usually leave when they are mature and wander alone, often for years, until they persuade females to join them and form a new group.

●Social insects

There are over 12,000 species of social insects, including all termites and some species of ants, bees and wasps. All have highly-organized societies. Termites live in vast groups called colonies. This is how many of these colonies are organized.

Termites build large mounds from earth mixed with saliva. Inside the mound is a nest full of chambers in which one family of over a million termites lives.

Chambers

Termite mound

The king and queen stay in a royal chamber deep inside the nest. They mate often. The queen may live many decades and acts as an egg-laying factory, producing as many as 36,000 eggs a day.

An old queen termite's abdomen may be 15cm (6 in) long and over 300 times its original size.

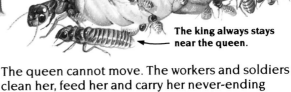

The king always stays near the queen.

Societies are made up of three groups, or castes: soldiers, workers, and reproductives (the king and queen who are the parents of all the termites). Each caste has a different body shape and does a different job. Workers are sterile (unable to breed) and blind. Their job is to care for the soldiers, the queen, the king and the young. They are the only caste able to break down food. They feed the others with regurgitated food.

The queen cannot move. The workers and soldiers clean her, feed her and carry her never-ending stream of eggs away to nursery chambers nearby.

The queen's attendants are rewarded by a sweet liquid, secreted from her abdomen.

Soldiers are also sterile. Their job is to defend the nest and its occupants and protect the workers on food-gathering trips.

The queen occasionally produces a chemical which makes the young develop sex organs. They then leave the nest and some pairs found new colonies.

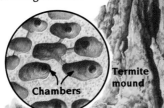

Worker feeding a soldier

Animal associations

It is not only members of the same species which live together. There are also close associations between members of two different species. These arrangements may benefit both animals in the association or only one. In some cases one species may harm or even kill the other.

Mutualism

Mutualism is the association of two species where both benefit. Some animals, for example, obtain food by removing parasites and insects from larger ones. The larger animals benefit by being cleaned.

Cleaner wrasses work in pairs in areas called "cleaning stations" in coral reefs. Larger fish visit these areas every few days to be cleaned. The wrasses first perform a dance to signal their identity so that the large fish do not eat them.

Cleaner wrasses remove dead skin, fungus and fish lice. They can deal with up to 50 customers an hour.

Cleaner shrimps also work at cleaning stations. They display to clients by waving their legs and antennae up and down.

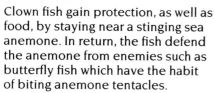

Oxpeckers search for food on zebras, giraffes, rhinos and other large mammals. Their claws are arranged in a way which allows them to run up and down the large animals' bodies.

Oxpecker

Oxpeckers remove fleas, ticks, and other parasites which the mammals could not remove themselves.

Galapagos giant tortoises are kept free of parasites by finches. A tortoise signals that it is ready to be cleaned by stretching its neck up and stiffening its legs, so that its shell is lifted up.

A giant tortoise stands motionless while a finch climbs over its body searching for parasites.

Clown fish gain protection, as well as food, by staying near a stinging sea anemone. In return, the fish defend the anemone from enemies such as butterfly fish which have the habit of biting anemone tentacles.

Clown fish are covered with a slime which seems to make them immune to their anemone's sting.

Some ant species "farm" herds of tiny insects called aphids. They protect their herds from predators, carry them to new food plants and prevent members from wandering away. In return, the aphids provide the ants with a sweet, liquid food called honeydew.

Ants make aphids release drops of honeydew by stroking them with their antennae. The honeydew is taken back to the ant colony.

Home sharing

Shearwaters in New Zealand often return from months at sea to find that their nest holes have been occupied by reptiles called tuataras. The tuataras keep the tunnels free of blockages, so that all the birds have to do is clear out the nest chamber at the far end.

●Commensalism

Commensalism is when one species in an association benefits by gaining food and sometimes shelter, and the other remains unaffected.

Cattle egrets stay near elephants, rhinos, and other large mammals. They eat ground-living insects disturbed by these animals' feet.

Raccoons come to cities to scavenge for food thrown out by humans. The humans remain unaffected by this.

●Parasitism

This is when one species (the parasite) gains at the expense of the other (the host). There are many types of parasites. Most do not kill their hosts, since to do so would reduce their own chances of survival.

Ectoparasites, such as fleas, are blood-suckers which live on the outside of their hosts.

Flea on a rabbit's ear

Endoparasites, such as tapeworms, live in their hosts' bodies, feeding off their food.

Tapeworms up to 2m (6 ft) long can live inside human intestines.

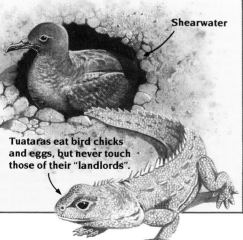

Shearwater

Tuataras eat bird chicks and eggs, but never touch those of their "landlords".

●Moving parasites

Some parasites move between two or more hosts to complete their life cycles. To do this, they may have to make a host change its behaviour. A kind of fluke that lives in the guts of birds passes its eggs out in their droppings. These may be eaten by a snail. They hatch into larvae and then become organisms called cysts. The cysts move to the snail's

Cysts in snail's tentacles

tentacles and make them throb. They also make the snail stay out in the open when it should be hiding. This attracts a bird which bites off the tentacles. In this way the parasite returns to its original host and completes its life cycle.

●Brood parasites

Cuckoos are brood parasites. A female lays up to 12 eggs, each in the nest of a smaller bird such as a warbler. She then abandons them.

A cuckoo's egg is similar in shape and size to the host's eggs.

When it hatches, the baby cuckoo pushes the other eggs out of the nest.

The baby is soon much larger than its "parents" and needs a lot of food.

●Parasitoids

Parasitoids lay their eggs in or on the body of another animal. When the eggs hatch, the larvae use the host as food, eating it from the inside. The vital organs are eaten last, so that the host stays alive as long as possible.

Wasp larvae fed on the inside of this caterpillar, then emerged to make these cocoons.

Cocoons

31

● Animal builders

Many animals are skilful builders. Most of their "buildings" are used as places to live and rear young, but some are designed to capture prey or to attract a mate. Spiders, insects and birds are the most skilled at building. Beavers are also well known for their building activities.

● Insect homes

Some insects, such as termites, build large, permanent homes. Others, such as wasps, make new nests every year.

Nigerian termites build huge mud mounds, made up of towers over underground nests. Each mound is the work of one family of over a million termites (see page 29) who regularly add to and repair their home.

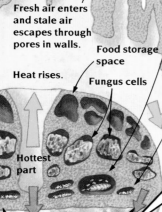

Tall, hollow towers with strong, hard walls may be over 6m (20 ft) tall.

Mound is made of tiny pellets of mud held together by termite saliva.

Inside the nest, the termites grow fungus to eat. This has to be kept at a temperature of 30-31°C (86-88°F). All the activity in the nest creates heat, so an "air-conditioning" system is built into the mound.

Royal cell contains queen and king.

Nursery cells contain eggs and larvae.

Warm, stale air from the nest rises up and then flows down flues (which run down the sides) to a large cellar below. As it flows, some air passes out through the porous walls and is replaced by fresh air.

Fresh air enters and stale air escapes through pores in walls.

Food storage space

Heat rises.

Fungus cells

Hottest part

Clay plate **Clay vanes**

Clay vanes

Cellar

Flue

Water seeps down.

Clay pillar supports nest.

The nest sits on a clay plate which soaks up water from above. On its underside are rings of clay vanes from which the water evaporates, cooling the air in the cellar before it enters the nest to circulate.

● Beaver constructions

Beavers change the environment to create their own living areas. They build dams across rivers and streams to widen them into ponds. These provide safe sites for their homes, which are called lodges.

A lodge is a pile of sticks, stones and mud with a single living chamber inside. Entrances are underwater, so food can be brought from a nearby food cache, even if the pond is frozen on top.

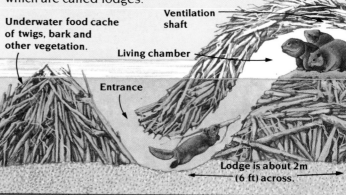

Underwater food cache of twigs, bark and other vegetation.

Ventilation shaft

Living chamber

Entrance

Lodge is about 2m (6 ft) across.

● Wasp nests

A common wasp nest begins as a pillar hanging from a roof or branch. Cells made of chewed wood are built up around it. A finished nest contains up to 15,000 cells in combs joined by struts.

Combs

Strut

Cells

Larvae are reared inside the cells.

Nest is about the size of a soccer ball.

A female potter wasp builds several jar-shaped mud nests. One egg is laid in each nest. Paralyzed caterpillars are put in as food for the larva when it hatches. The jar is then sealed.

Potter wasp laying a single egg in her nest.

The dam is begun with stones and built up with sticks, logs and mud. The beavers fell trees into the water, gnaw them to shorter lengths and then tow them to the dam.

The dam is extended year after year. It may be up to 550m (600yds) long and 1.5m (5 ft) high.

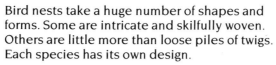

Bird nests

Bird nests take a huge number of shapes and forms. Some are intricate and skilfully woven. Others are little more than loose piles of twigs. Each species has its own design.

A pair of storks makes a large nest of sticks on the top of a chimney. They nest at the same site every year.

White-capped albatrosses make tube-shaped nests about 30cm (1 ft) tall.

An ovenbird's nest is a dome made of mud, hairs and vegetable fibres.

Cup-shaped nests are very common. Blue grosbeaks build theirs from twigs, leaves, paper and snakeskins.

Nest-building is instinctive – even a bird raised away from its parents can make its species' nest without help, but it does need to practise before it can make a perfect nest.

Male weaverbirds knot and weave grasses together using their feet and beaks. A young bird's first attempts are often unsuccessful.

A masked weaverbird's nest starts as a series of loops of grass tied firmly to a branch.

Weaverbird with completed nest awaiting a mate. Females inspect nests carefully when choosing a mate, so nest-building ability helps determine breeding success.

Building attractions

Each spring, male bowerbirds make stick bowers and decorate them solely to attract females. They improve their bowers daily and are always on the look-out for ornaments, often stealing them from rivals. The males with the finest bowers attract most females.

A satin bowerbird displays his treasures in front of his bower. Anything blue is suitable for this species.

When a female approaches, the male performs a courtship display. If she is impressed, and mating takes place, the female builds a simple cup-shaped nest near the bower and raises the young by herself.

Capturing prey

Many spiders spin webs to catch food. When an insect gets caught in the threads, the spider rushes out, delivers a poisonous bite to the victim and wraps up the body as a meal for later. Webs seldom last longer than one night. Damaged ones are rolled up and eaten by the spider.

Webs are made from a silk-like protein produced from a spider's abdomen.

Courtship and mating

The term courtship is used to describe all the activities that precede mating. Courtship behaviour varies widely from species to species. For some it is just a question of meeting and mating. Others have special ways of attracting a mate, using calls, colours or smells or by performing complex displays.

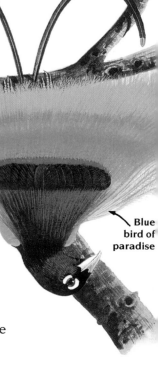

Hedgehogs meet by chance. The male circles around the female to signal his intentions. She may reject him many times before mating finally occurs.

Courtship displays

Courtship is a time of stress. Females tend to be frightened and males become aggressive. Displays which precede mating in many species are designed not only to attract a mate, but to suppress fear and aggression and to aid recognition, making sure both animals are of the same species.

Male sticklebacks acquire special colours and females develop a rounded, silvery appearance for the breeding season. These changes affect the behaviour of each sex.

A male waits by the nest he has built. When a female comes near, he swims towards her and does a dance.

This encourages the female to approach and show her swollen belly.

He recognizes this signal and swims towards the nest.

The female follows and he indicates the entrance of the nest with special movements.

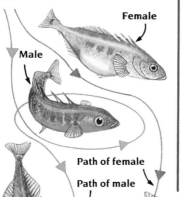

Male

Female

Path of female

Path of male

When the female enters, he nudges her tail and waggles his body. As she leaves she lays eggs.

The male then swims through the nest and sheds sperm over the eggs to fertilize them. He then loses his bright colours and takes care of the eggs.

Bird displays

Many male birds, often equipped with brightly-coloured feathers or inflatable air sacs, perform energetic displays to try to impress females.

A blue bird of paradise performs an upside-down display, vibrating his plumage and letting his tail plumes fall into a graceful curve. After the breeding season, the tail plumes are moulted.

When a male magnificent frigatebird is ready to court, his orange throat pouch turns bright red. He collects sticks to make a nest on which he performs. If a female is interested, she offers him more sticks. After mating, one egg is laid and both birds look after the egg and chick.

Blue bird of paradise

A frigatebird inflates his throat pouch, claps his bill and takes up a number of different poses to try to attract a mate.

Meeting places

Frogs and toads return to the same place each year to mate and lay eggs.

Male golden toads gather at the edge of a tiny pool, waiting for their bright colours to attract females. They are unusual since they do not call to advertise for mates.

When a female arrives, the males swarm over her, pushing and shoving to try to get a chance to mate.

●Courtship dances

In some species, both male and female display, performing a dance which may last many hours. These dances establish pair bonds and bring both animals into a similar emotional state, so that mating can occur.

All species of cranes engage in courtship dances during the breeding season. Japanese cranes sing duets as they perform.

The dance starts slowly with the birds bowing to each other and turning with delicate steps.

As the dance goes on, they become more excited, flapping their wings and leaping up to 3m (10 ft) into the air.

After mating, the pair build a large nest of twigs and reeds and share the care of the eggs and the young.

The males of some bird species give the female a courtship gift which shows their intention to mate. This is either a piece of food or nesting material.

A bee-eater presents his mate with a dragonfly as a courtship gift.

●Dangerous liaisons

For some male animals, mating can be a risky business, since their potential mates could injure or even kill them. They have ways of getting round this problem, however.

A female scorpion has large claws and a poisonous tail. A male must take care to avoid being eaten. He grabs her claws in his own and does a dance with her. This clears the area so that he can deposit his sperm on the ground. He then manoeuvres her over the sperm and she takes it up. Only then will he release her.

A scorpion mating dance may last many hours.

Courting hares often engage in boxing matches. A match continues until the male gives up or is injured, or the female gets hurt or allows the male to mate with her.

Hares in boxing match

Female

In some species, mating takes place each year at a communal site called a "lek". The males fight to claim the most prized areas in the middle of the lek.

Up to 100 male topi (a type of antelope) travel to a lek each year. Females make their way to the middle to mate with the most senior male. Younger males seldom get a chance to mate.

Rival topi meet at the boundaries of their areas and perform ritualized threat displays.

● Fatal attraction

In some species of praying mantis, the female eats the male while they are mating. She starts at his head and by the time she reaches his abdomen, mating is completed.

Female

Male's head

Male's body

● Breeding and rearing young

The amount of time and effort parents spend on rearing their young varies greatly from species to species. Generally, those which produce a large number of eggs or young have nothing, or little, to do with their development, but a few still survive to reach adulthood. Species which produce only a few offspring or eggs at a time need to protect their young carefully to ensure their survival.

Swallowtail butterfly
Egg
Larva

Insects, such as butterflies, often lay eggs on a food plant suitable for the hatching larvae to feed on, but the rest is left to chance.

Nile crocodile hatching

A female Nile crocodile lays eggs in a pit which she digs on a sandy river bank. She guards her nest carefully for 6-14 weeks, driving off predators and awaiting the croaking sounds from inside the eggs which signal that the babies are ready to hatch. She then digs them out of the ground. When they have hatched, the mother may carry each baby to the water in her mouth. She continues guarding them as they grow and develop.

● Carrying eggs and young

A male midwife toad mates with a number of females, taking from each a strand of eggs which he wraps around his back legs. He carries them like this for several weeks and then deposits them in a pond where they hatch.

Midwife toad

An arrow-poison frog transports his tadpoles on his back up to a bromeliad plant on a tree. The leaves of the plant form a cup in which rainwater collects. The tadpoles develop into frogs in this mini-pond.

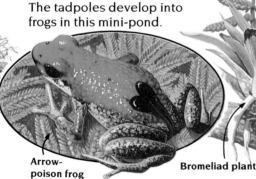

Arrow-poison frog

Bromeliad plant

Many species of cichlid fish keep their eggs in their mouths. When the young hatch, they stay in their mother's mouth for safety until they can look after themselves.

Young cichlids dart back inside their mother's mouth when danger threatens.

● Breeding birds

Some birds are hatched at an advanced stage and need little care from their parents, but most are helpless and have to be kept warm, clean and well fed.

A male mallee fowl builds a nest made up of a pit filled with rotting vegetation, covered with sand. The vegetation heats up and the male digs a hole in which the hen lays an egg. She then lays one egg a week for six months.

Pit is 60-90cm (2-3 ft) deep and 3m (10ft) wide.

A mallee fowl tests the temperature with his beak. By removing or replacing sand, he keeps the nest at 33°C (91°F).

When the young mallee fowl hatch, they are ignored by the parents and have to fend for themselves. They can run and find food within hours and can fly when only a day old.

Young roseate spoonbills stay in the nest for about six weeks. Both parents care for them. The young have to practise flying and learn to feed themselves when they leave.

Young spoonbills reach into an adult's throat for partly-digested food.

A female emperor penguin lays a single egg which is then passed to the male. For two months he carries it on his feet under a flap of skin, for warmth. The female returns to the sea to feed, but returns for hatching and to look after the young.

Newly-hatched emperor penguins are kept warm on their parents' feet.

● Mammal parents

Baby mammals need long periods of parental care. They are totally dependent on their mother for milk and are looked after almost exclusively by her. She licks the newborn babies clean, and if prevented from doing this, she may reject them. The period of parental care is longest in primates and large carnivores, such as tigers, and shortest in small insectivores, such as shrews.

A foraging white-toothed shrew takes her young with her when they are only 7 days old. Each shrew holds on to the one in front. When they are 3 weeks old they can look after themselves.

A tigress gives birth to up to seven cubs inside a den, but usually only two or three survive. The newborn cubs are helpless and spend eight weeks in the den, feeding on their mother's milk. She keeps them warm and licks them often.

Nuzzling reinforces family bonds and provides security for tiger cubs who compete constantly for their mother's attention.

At first, the mother keeps the cubs hidden when she goes hunting, but when they are about three months old, she leads them to a kill. She teaches them everything they need to know to survive, but they cannot fend for themselves until they are two years old and have learned how to hunt.

● Babies in pouches

A newborn kangaroo creeps through its mother's fur to reach her pouch where it spends four months feeding from a teat. From then on it will sometimes stick its head out and soon begins to leave the pouch for short periods.

A kangaroo is less than 2.5cm (1in) long at birth.

A baby kangaroo, or "joey", always jumps back inside its mother's pouch if in danger or when tired.

A baby koala stays in its mother's pouch for six months. It spends the next six months riding on her back, feeding over her shoulder on leaves.

Baby koala

● Play

As in humans, play is an important part of learning for young animals. Playing with brothers and sisters and with parents helps them to learn about efficient ways of moving about, catching prey and escaping from enemies.

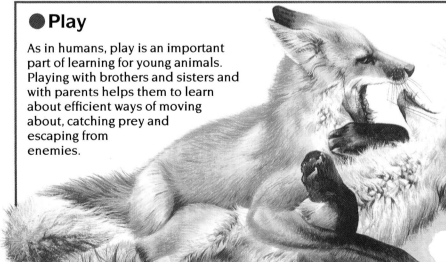

Play-fighting helps young foxes develop survival skills they will need in later life.

Playing 'king-of-the-castle' helps a young goat develop its sense of balance and climbing ability.

Rhythms and cycles

Animals have developed patterns of behaviour which run in rhythms and cycles in order to cope with changes in their environment on a yearly, monthly, daily, or even more short-term basis.

Rhythms and cycles are series of events which are repeated at regular or fairly regular intervals, in the same order. They can be understood by observing the way animals behave over a period of time.

Circannual cycles

In most parts of the world, the temperature and availability of food vary with the seasons. Animals adjust to this by organizing much of their behaviour in circannual cycles – cycles of about a year. For example, they may hibernate (see page 39) or migrate to avoid exposure to cold weather, and time their breeding activities to take advantage of good weather.

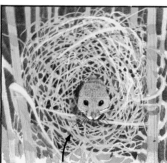

Between April and September each year, a harvest mouse takes advantage of good food supplies to raise several litters inside her nest.

In many cases it is not fully understood how animals "know" the best time for certain activities. Some activities are governed by external conditions such as changes in temperature or day length, others by some sort of internal clock. Day length changes are known to trigger bird migrations.

As the days grow shorter, white storks flock together from widespread summer breeding grounds in Europe to migrate to Africa for the winter.

Increasing or decreasing day length also brings about changes in the appearance of certain animals which need to be camouflaged against a background of snow.

At the end of summer, a stoat grows white fur for winter camouflage. Its brown fur returns in spring as the days lengthen.

Breeding changes

Reproductive development and breeding behaviour also occur on a circannual basis. For animals which breed in the spring, increasing day length may stimulate the development of breeding colours and activities.

Puffins grow large, brightly-coloured bills for the breeding season. These are used for digging burrows and in courtship. After breeding, their bills become smaller and less colourful.

Each spring, sage grouse gather to display at their breeding grounds. They fan their tails, fluff up their feathers and inflate and deflate their air sacs with loud popping sounds.

Moulting behaviour

Birds moult once or twice a year – their flight feathers drop out and are replaced. Ducks, swans and geese lose all theirs at once. This affects their behaviour since they cannot fly for a short period and so are vulnerable to attack.

During moulting, shelducks stay in the middle of an expanse of water or on a mudflat so they can spot predators from a long way off.

● Hibernation and aestivation

Some animals conserve energy to survive the winter by going into hibernation for many months. This is a sleep-like state in which breathing and heartbeat rate slow down and body temperature falls as low as 2°C (35°F). Some animals in hot climates respond to heat and drought in the summer by going into a similar sleep-like state called aestivation.

Between October and April, a European hedgehog hibernates inside its burrow. Its heartbeat drops from over 180 to 20 beats a minute. Its temperature falls from 35°C (95°F) to as low as 4°C (40°F).

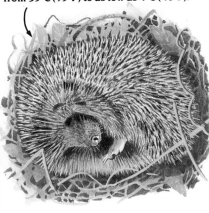

When lakes dry up in the dry season, an African lungfish burrows into the mud and forms a protective cocoon around its body from hardened mucus.

Inside its cocoon, it aestivates until it rains again, breathing air which filters down through cracks in the mud.

● Lunar cycles

A number of animals respond to the lunar (moon) cycle of 29.5 days. The most famous is the palolo worm in coral reefs in the Pacific Ocean. On the first day of the last quarter of the moon in October or November, the bottom parts of all the worms break off, rise to the surface and release eggs and sperm so that fertilization takes place.

It is not known how the worms judge the phases of the moon. They spawn (produce eggs and sperm) even when the sky is overcast. Worms on reefs as much as 965km (600 miles) apart spawn at the same time.

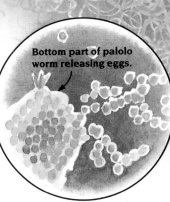

Bottom part of palolo worm releasing eggs.

● Circadian rhythms

Most animals respond to changes in environmental conditions between night and day. Different animals have to be awake and alert at the "right" times for them, whether this is day, night, dawn or dusk. For the majority, the circadian (daily) rhythm of activities is designed to make the best use of opportunities to find food.

Animals specialized for daytime vision cannot forage at night and are in danger from predators. Sleeping in a safe place helps them save energy and avoid enemies.

Red squirrels sleep in dreys (nests made of twigs and leaves) at night. From dawn to dusk they are busy looking for food.

Nocturnal animals sleep during the day and take advantage of their night vision as well as particular conditions (such as cooler temperatures in deserts) to forage or hunt at night.

Badgers leave their underground homes at sunset to go foraging.

Some small mammals, such as moles, show rhythms of activity over periods of a few hours. These are known as sub-circadian rhythms.

Daily rhythms of activities may be altered by learning. Birds and bees, for example, may learn at what times humans provide food.

Many gulls have learned to time their feeding activities to coincide with the arrival of trucks at waste tips.

Circadian rhythms seem to be controlled by internal clocks as much as by external conditions. Chicks, mice and lizards reared in conditions where temperature and light remain constant show normal circadian rhythms from an early age.

Behaviour under extreme conditions

Various species live in conditions of extreme heat, cold or in total darkness, in deserts, polar regions, oceans and caves, or on mountains. Special types of behaviour, as well as physical adaptations (such as thick fur in cold climates) allow them to survive in these habitats.

Surviving in the desert

The temperature in deserts can reach over 50°C (120°F) during the day and water is nearly always scarce. Desert animals have to keep cool without losing too much water by evaporation. They use a variety of methods to do this. Sheltering underground or in the shade is one of the most common.

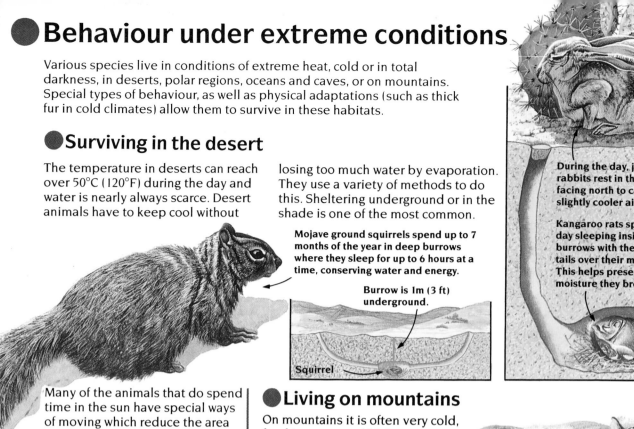

Mojave ground squirrels spend up to 7 months of the year in deep burrows where they sleep for up to 6 hours at a time, conserving water and energy.

Burrow is 1m (3 ft) underground.

Squirrel

During the day, jack rabbits rest in the shade, facing north to catch the slightly cooler air.

Kangaroo rats spend the day sleeping inside sealed burrows with their bushy tails over their mouths. This helps preserve the moisture they breathe out.

Many of the animals that do spend time in the sun have special ways of moving which reduce the area of the body in contact with the hot surface of the sand.

Fringe-toed lizards stand on two legs at a time to keep cool.

The sandfish (a type of lizard) can "swim" through the sand just below the surface.

Many desert snakes use a "sidewinding" movement to get about. Only two places near the head and tail touch the sand.

Living on mountains

On mountains it is often very cold, food is scarce and high wind speeds cause rapid evaporation of water. These are some of the ways animals survive in these harsh conditions.

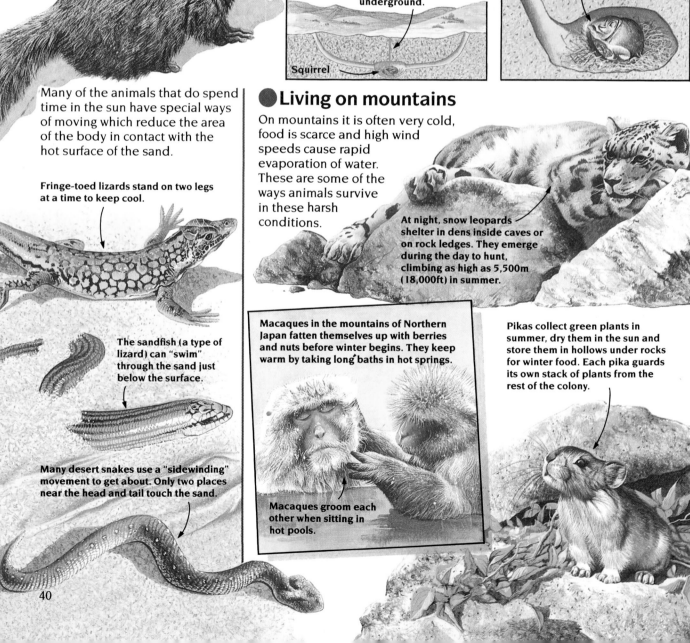

At night, snow leopards shelter in dens inside caves or on rock ledges. They emerge during the day to hunt, climbing as high as 5,500m (18,000ft) in summer.

Macaques in the mountains of Northern Japan fatten themselves up with berries and nuts before winter begins. They keep warm by taking long baths in hot springs.

Macaques groom each other when sitting in hot pools.

Pikas collect green plants in summer, dry them in the sun and store them in hollows under rocks for winter food. Each pika guards its own stack of plants from the rest of the colony.

●Polar regions

In the polar regions, the temperature may fall as low as −80°C (−112°F) in winter. Staying under the snow where the temperature rarely drops below −7°C (19°F) is one method of surviving the winter.

A female polar bear and her cubs spend the coldest months of the year in a den dug in a snow drift.

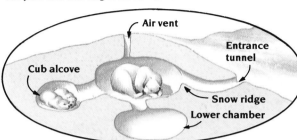

Air vent

Entrance tunnel

Cub alcove

Snow ridge

Lower chamber

Seals keep breathing holes open in the ice. Polar bears locate the seals by scent and wait by the holes for them to appear. They also break open the ice to capture seal pups.

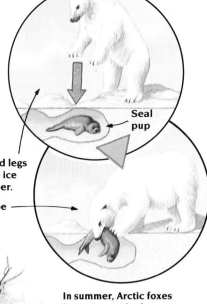

Seal pup

A polar bear rears up on its hind legs before crashing down on to the ice above a seal pup's birth chamber.

The pup is pulled out by a swipe of the paw and then grabbed by the jaws.

Food is very scarce when the ground and sea are frozen and covered in snow. Many animals have developed ingenious methods of getting food.

Cross foxes sniff out lemmings under the snow and kill them by springing high into the air and coming down hard enough to break through the ice crust on to a lemming below.

In summer, Arctic foxes bury eggs and other foods in the thawed surface layer of the tundra. They dig out their deep-frozen caches in winter.

●Life in the twilight zones

No light penetrates the sea below 900m (3,000 feet). Most fish living below this depth make their own. They also have specialized ways of finding food.

The viper fish, a fierce predator, produces light from organs containing luminous cells. Lights inside its mouth help to lure fish into its jaws.

Gulper eels hunt by swimming with their mouths wide open. They depend on smell and sensing vibrations in the water to find prey.

In the darkness of caves, animals rely on senses other than sight to navigate and find food. Some have reduced vision or are blind.

Blind cave characins in underwater caves in Mexico have lost their power of sight. They find food and avoid obstacles by sensing vibrations in the water.

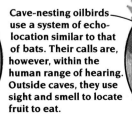

Cave-nesting oilbirds use a system of echo-location similar to that of bats. Their calls are, however, within the human range of hearing. Outside caves, they use sight and smell to locate fruit to eat.

Taming and farming animals

The taming of wild animals began over 10,000 years ago, when people were still hunters and gatherers, travelling around in small family groups. Since that time, animals have been used for food, transport, work and as pets.

The taming process

Animals that lived in packs, herds or groups were easiest to tame as they transferred a dependence on the leader of their group to a dependence on a human. The very first animals to be domesticated were dogs.

Most people believe that dogs are descended from a small race of Asiatic wolves.

Wolves were killed by human hunters because they competed for the same prey. The first pet "dogs" were probably orphaned wolf cubs brought back after a hunt. They responded to kindness and were tamed by gentle handling and constant exposure to people. From then on they were taken around from place to place.

Wolf cub

Much later, the process of selective breeding began, whereby animals with similar traits were bred together to produce offspring suitable for particular purposes such as guarding, hunting or herding. This has continued until the present day when there are more than 400 dog breeds with a great variety of characteristics.

Dogs are still used by hunters to retrieve game.

Dogs still retain elements of wolf behaviour, such as scent marking, and territorial fighting. They will still readily form packs, and puppies will become wild if isolated from people.

Admirable cats

Pet cats are descended from races of wildcat, probably African wildcats. Their first known contact with man seems to have been about 4,500 years ago in Egypt. The Egyptians admired the wildcats which hunted rats in their granaries and began to tame and train them to fish and hunt. Eventually cats were promoted to the level of goddesses.

African wildcat

Bronze figure of the Egyptian goddess Bast.

Modern pet cats have lost much of their savagery but they remain solitary hunters. Their hunting methods (see page 22) are the same as those of their wild ancestors.

Farm animals

The first animals to be herded were goats and sheep. Nomadic hunters took their herds from one place to another.

Goats were domesticated 9,000-10,000 years ago from wild bezoar goats of what is now Israel, Iran and Jordan.

Sheep are descended from wild sheep called mouflon. They were kept first for meat and milk, not wool.

The thick wool of modern sheep is a result of selective breeding.

Pigs were not domesticated until people began settling in villages and growing crops. The pig's ability to produce a lot of young and live on almost anything edible led to its popularity.

All pigs are descended from wild boar which still live in forests. Females produce up to 12 young in a litter.

As result of selective breeding, a modern pig may weigh twice as much as a wild boar and give birth to up to 20 piglets in a litter.

Chickens are descended from red jungle fowl. A wild fowl lays about 30 eggs a year, but if her nest is robbed repeatedly, she lays as many as 80. Observation of this behaviour made people realize that the fowl would be good food producers if domesticated.

Red jungle fowl were first domesticated in India and China about 4,000 years ago.

Chickens retain many of the traits of their ancestors such as a pecking order within groups (see page 13). A modern hen may lay as many as 300 eggs a year

It is not known when cattle were first domesticated, though it was later than sheep and goats. Most modern cattle are descended from aurochs – large, fierce wild cattle which once lived in herds in parts of Europe, Asia and North Africa. Cattle were kept for their meat, skin, milk, fat, horn and bone.

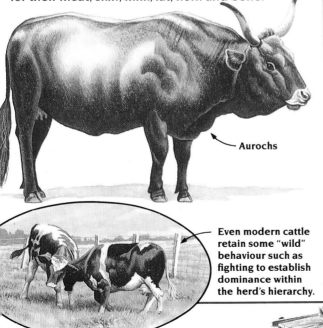

Aurochs

Even modern cattle retain some "wild" behaviour such as fighting to establish dominance within the herd's hierarchy.

Horses and donkeys

The donkey's capacity for carrying heavy loads has been recognized for thousands of years. The ancestor of the donkey is the Nubian Ass.

Nubian ass

Przewalski's horse

Horses were first kept in the Ukraine region of the USSR about 5,500 years ago. They probably looked similar to Przewalski's horses which can still be seen in zoos.

Ancestral values

Animals which man has domesticated in harsh conditions such as deserts, mountains and polar regions remain similar to their ancestors, as their value lies in their ability to survive in these habitats.

Camels can go for a long time without water in the desert. They are used for transport and to provide milk, meat, hide and hair.

Yaks thrive in the thin air and bitter cold of the Himalayas. They are sturdy pack animals and also provide rich milk, meat, wool and hide which is used to make tents.

Reindeer in polar and tundra regions have been herded since the end of the last ice age. They were first exploited for meat, hide and horns and much later used to carry loads and for transport.

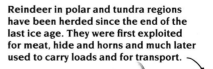

Using and training animals

People have made use of domesticated animals for far more than just food and farm work. Animals can be trained to perform a wide variety of tasks and to take part in many different sports and leisure activities. All of these involve close co-operation with humans.

Working dogs

Dogs are used in a number of ways. Guide dogs, for example, are trained to be a blind person's 'eyes'.

Potential guide dogs must be strong, healthy, obedient, intelligent and must show no nervousness. Puppies are given specialist care from birth. Serious training begins when a dog is a year old and takes at least six months, during which dogs have to learn to guide their trainer safely across roads, cope with public transport, escalators, revolving doors, crowded streets and so on.

A guide dog and its owner are carefully matched and go through a period of training together. Eventually they establish a close bond and friendship.

Dogs which are used to herd animals have to be able to to drive and control large herds by "persuading" them to move in certain directions, without biting or attacking them. They also need an ability to respond to a number of commands.

Sheep dogs are trained to follow whistled and shouted commands from a shepherd.

Dogs used to be used extensively for hauling loads. In the Arctic, they were the only means of transport for thousands of years. Sled dogs can survive on frozen scraps of food and sleep in hollows scraped out from the frozen ground.

Sled dogs →

Dogs are also used by the police, customs officials, rescue services and armed forces for tasks such as sniffing out drugs, detecting people trapped under snow, and tracking. Handlers train their own dog so that handler and dog build up a high level of trust.

The German Shepherd's intelligence, strength and ability to be trained make them the most popular choice as police and army dogs. They are also used as guide, guard and rescue dogs.

A German Shepherd showing off its skills at a display.

More useful workers

A number of other animals also perform useful tasks for humans.

Capuchin monkeys, for example, can be trained to help disabled people, performing tasks such as brushing hair, opening doors, retrieving objects, doing simple housework and serving food.

This woman gives her monkey instructions by means of a mouth-operated laser pen.

In some places, the pig's keen sense of smell and instinctive rooting behaviour have enabled them to be trained to sniff out truffles (delicious wild fungi which grow underground).

Pig sniffing out truffles

Sea-lions are trained to take and retrieve tools from divers working on the sea-bed.

Sports and pastimes

Many sports or pastimes which involve animals have developed from hunting or military activities.

Falconry

The art of falconry has been carried on in Asia for more than 4,000 years and is still widely practised there today. It spread to Europe about 1,500 years ago. Training a falcon to catch birds in flight and return to a falconer takes a lot of time and patience.

A young bird is hooded to keep it calm and has straps attached to its legs. The falconer carries the bird around on his gloved fist for long periods to get it used to being handled. At first the bird is allowed to fly short distances on a leash. Eventually it is trained to catch a lure (a dummy bird on a string) and then small birds.

Falcon

Pigeon racing

The Egyptians used pigeons to send military messages as long ago as 1204BC and pigeons were still used for this purpose up until fairly recently. Now the pigeon's homing ability (see page 17) is used in racing.

Pigeons are trained by being released at increasing distances from their home loft. Selective breeding has produced birds that can fly at 96km (60 miles) per hour.

Equestrianism

Equestrianism (the art of horsemanship) involves activities such as show jumping and dressage and requires close co-operation between horse and rider.

Dressage can be seen in its most advanced form in the Spanish Riding School in Vienna, where horses are trained to perform intricate, dance-like movements.

Talking with animals

Many attempts have been made by humans to communicate with animals. Some people have taught gorillas and chimps American Sign Language (ASL), as used by deaf and dumb people, by repeatedly moulding their hands to the correct shapes.

A gorilla named Koko began learning ASL in 1972 and now knows over 1,000 words. She also understands spoken English. A chimp called Washoe who was learning ASL also taught over 50 words to her son.

Koko described her kitten as a "soft good cat cat".

Studies have also been done with chimps using lexigrams – boards with 256 symbols on them, each symbol representing a word. Researchers touch the symbols to create simple sentences, speaking at the same time.

A chimp called Kanzi has been learning this system since he was six months old. He has picked up 200 words, often combining them with gestures to make short sentences. His understanding of speech is, however, much greater and he can follow complicated instructions.

Chimp using lexigram to "talk" to a researcher.

45

● Important people in the study of behaviour

Charles Darwin (1809-1882)

The founder of the theory of evolution by natural selection which explained how plants and animals have gradually changed into different kinds of plants and animals over a long period of time and that those individuals best adapted to their environment survive to pass on their characteristics. His book *On the Origin of Species* (1859) had an enormous influence on the study of behaviour. Before Darwin, animals were thought of as separate from intelligent humans. In *The Descent of Man* (1871), Darwin stressed similarities between animal and human behaviour and showed how animals were adapted behaviourally and physically.

Henri Fabré (1823-1915)

The first man to make detailed observations of animals in their natural surroundings and record what he saw. He spent 40 years watching insects in his garden in France and astonished the world with evidence of how complex insect behaviour is.

Ivan Pavlov (1849-1936)

Russian physiologist best known for his studies on conditioned reflexes which have provided the basis for much research into how animals learn (see page 8). His research was based on controlled experiments in laboratories.

Karl von Frisch (1886-1982)

Austrian zoologist, spent most of his life in Germany. His main interest was in finding out how animals obtain infomation about their environment. His most famous discovery was that bees inform each other of the whereabouts of food by dances (see page 19). In 1973 he shared a Nobel Prize with Lorenz and Tinbergen for his contribution to the development of ethology.

Konrad Lorenz (1903-1989)

Austrian zoologist, has been called 'the father of modern ethology'. Through his observation of greylag geese and many other species, he founded a theory of instinct, making a distinction between an animal's observable activity (its behaviour pattern) and the internal processes which bring the activity about (its motivation). He identified the phenomenon of imprinting in young chicks (see page 4). In later work he explored the roots of human aggression.

Nikolaas Tinbergen (1907-1988)

Dutch zoologist. His studies were done mainly with animals in the wild. Much of his research was concerned with how animals find their way around their environment and he designed many experiments to investigate this, such as one to find out how a digger wasp recognizes her burrow (see page 5). He also studied behaviour in sticklebacks and gulls. Later, he used methods derived from ethology to study human behaviour.

Burrhus Frederick Skinner (1904-1990)

American psychologist. He made detailed studies of learning with animals in captivity. He perfected a device (the Skinner box – see page 9) in which animals were taught by reinforcing certain actions, such as pressing levers, with food as a reward when the correct result was achieved. He believed that these principles of conditioned behaviour could also be applied to humans.

Dian Fossey (1932-1985)

American physiotherapist who earned fame by living among mountain gorillas on the slopes of the Viruga Volcanoes in Central Africa. Following up the work of the scientist George Schaller, she gained the gorillas' confidence and so was able to observe them over a long period. Her work did much to dispel the myth of gorillas as monsters and showed that they are in fact gentle, intelligent vegetarians with complex behaviour patterns and social structures.

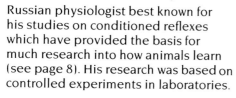

Jane Goodall (born 1934)

Jane Goodall began her now famous study of the lives of wild chimpanzees at Tanzania's Gombe National Park in 1960. It took her a year to gain the chimps' trust before she could observe them at close quarters. She shocked the scientific world with her discovery that chimps hunt and eat meat and are intelligent enough to make and use tools (see page 11). Before this it had been believed that tool-making was solely a human skill. Her findings have been an important influence on the work of other ethologists.

Glossary

Aestivation. Sleep-like state some animals enter into during the summer to conserve energy and water and survive heat and drought.

Associative learning. Also called **Learning by association.** Type of learning in which an animal associates (links together) two or more sets of circumstances or stimuli.

Brood parasitism. Breeding system in which an animal puts its eggs into the nest of another species and lets its young be raised by the host species.

Camouflage. Colouring or patterning which allows an animal to blend with its background and so avoid being seen by predators. An animal must keep very still for camouflage to be effective.

Caste. Members of a species adapted physically and behaviourally to perform specific tasks.

Circadian rhythm. Rhythm of about one day in length according to which many animals organize their behaviour.

Circannual cycle. Cycle of about one year in length according to which many animals organize patterns of behaviour.

Commensalism. Association between two species in which one species benefits and the other remains unaffected.

Conflict behaviour. Behaviour which results from an animal being "torn" between two conflicting urges.

Co-operative behaviour. Also called **Co-operation.** System in which members of a species join together and assist each other in activities such as care of young, feeding and hunting.

Courtship. All the activities, such as displays, presentation of courtship gifts, and mate selection, that precede mating.

Displacement activity. Activity, such as preening during a fight, which seems irrelevant to the situation in which it occurs.

Display. Pattern of movement used as part of communication, especially during courtship and in aggressive behaviour.

Habituation. Type of learning in which, over a ▶ period of time, an animal gets used to a stimulus which is presented to it repeatedly, (but which is neither dangerous nor rewarding) and ceases to respond to it.

Hibernation. Sleep-like state which some animals enter into during the winter months to conserve energy and survive periods of low temperature and food scarcity.

Imitation. Learning in which one animal learns by copying another.

Imprinting. Process in which newborn animals "fix upon" and learn the characteristics of another animal (usually a parent).

Insight. Learning which involves the appreciation of complex relationships and a process of mental reasoning.

Latent learning. Process of "taking in" information without actively learning it, and using it at a later time.

Lek. Area in which the males of certain species hold small territories during the breeding season in which they perform displays to try to attract a mate.

Lunar cycle. Cycle of 29.5 days, corresponding to a cycle of the moon, according to which a few animals organize their behaviour.

Migration. Long distance movements between one place and ▶ another, shown by many species.

Mimicry. Resemblance in appearance or behaviour between animals of different species which benefits one or both.

Mobbing. Response shown by some animals, especially small birds, to a potential predator, in which they collectively attack or threaten to attack it.

Mutualism. Association between two species which benefits both.

Parasitism. Association between two animals in which one species (the parasite) gains at the expense of the other (the host).

Pecking order. Ranking of members in a social group such that each one knows its position and will dominate all below it.

Redirected response. Response directed to external stimuli which are irrelevant to the current situation, e.g a gull pulling at grass instead of an opponent's wing during a fight.

Spatial learning. Learning the positions of objects in an area.

Stotting. Performance of high, stiff-legged leaps by gazelles that have spotted a predator.

Sub-circadian rhythm. Rhythm of a few hours in length, according to which some animals organize their behaviour.

Territory. Area occupied by an animal or group of animals.

Warning colours. Body colouring or patterning which warns predators that an animal can sting, is poisonous, etc.

Index